Here's what kids
have to say to Ro
the **A to Z Mysteries** series:

Whenever I go to the library, I always get
an A to Z Mystery. It doesn't matter if I
have read it a hundred times. I never get
tired of reading them!—Kristen M.

I love your books. You have quite a talent to
write A to Z Mysteries. I like to think I am
Dink. RON ROY ROCKS!—Patrick P.

I love your A to Z Mysteries. They're really
good. I love reading and hope to write
books myself someday.—Eva Z.

I could not put *The Absent Author* down!
—Mandy G.

Nothing can tear me away from
your books!—Rachel O.

Every time I have a free minute I sit down
and read your books.—Emily C.

Thank you for your wonderful books,
Mr. Roy. Ryan has always enjoyed reading,
but this is amazing. In one day he read all
of D and E and got a good start on F. He
just can't put them down.—Mrs. V.

ISBN 0-439-33293-1

12 11 10 9 18 17 16 15 14 13   5 6 7/0

Printed in the U.S.A.   40

First Scholastic printing, March 2002

A to Z Mysteries

The Lucky Lottery

by **Ron Roy**

illustrated by
John Steven Gurney

SCHOLASTIC INC.

New York   Toronto   London   Auckland   Sydney
Mexico City   New Delhi   Hong Kong   Buenos Aires

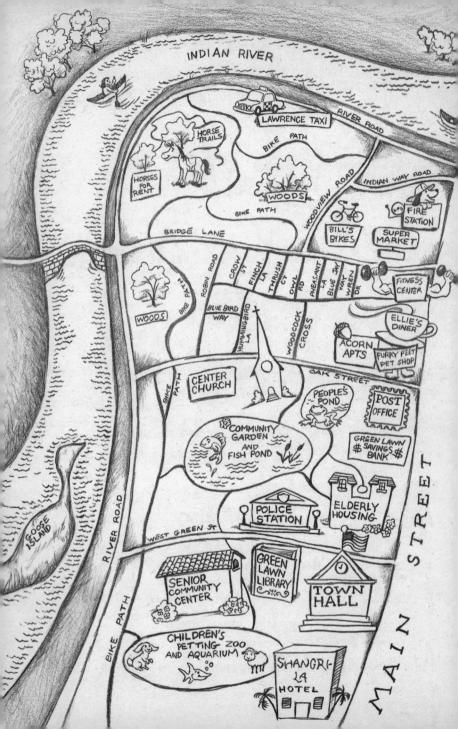

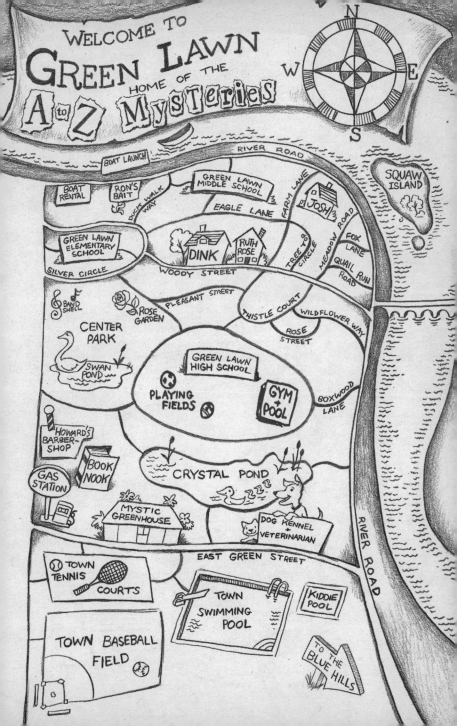

CHAPTER 1

"READY, AIM, FIRE!" yelled Ruth Rose.

She and Dink hurled snowballs at Josh's fort.

Josh's grinning face popped up. "Missed by a mile!" he yelled. "You throw like a girl, Ruth Rose!"

"I *am* a girl!" Ruth Rose yelled back. She whipped another snowball, catching Josh in the face.

The sides were uneven, but no one

cared. It was Dink, Ruth Rose, and her little brother, Nate, against Josh and his dog, Pal.

Nate was in charge of making snowballs for his sister and Dink. Pal raced around barking and trying to catch the snowballs in his mouth.

More snowballs flew at Josh's fort. Suddenly, Dink yelled, "Stop!"

Two little kids in lumpy snowsuits had wandered into Dink's backyard.

"Who're they?" asked Ruth Rose.

Dink shrugged. He and Ruth Rose dropped their snowballs and walked over to the newcomers.

The taller one was a boy. He wore a dark blue parka and a green ski hat. The shorter one was a girl. Her red hair framed blue eyes and pink cheeks.

"Hi," Dink said. "Who're you?"

"I'm Josephine!" the girl said.

"And I'm Ben," the boy said. "We

brought you a message from our big brother."

Josh climbed out of his fort and walked over. "Who's your brother?" he asked.

"Lucky O'Leary!" Josephine said.

"Oh, now I recognize you," Ruth Rose said. "You live over on Robin Road."

Ben O'Leary unzipped his parka pocket and pulled out a crumpled note. "Here, Lucky said to read it right now." He handed the note to Dink.

Dink flattened out the paper.

Guys, I need you.
Come to my house now. Urgent!
Lucky

"Did Lucky say what this is about?" Dink asked.

"It's a secret!" Josephine said, her eyes wide.

Dink, Josh, and Ruth Rose looked at each other.

"Let's go!" Ruth Rose said. She pointed her brother toward their house. "Nate, please go stay with Mom. Tell her I had to go on a secret mission!"

Dink, Josh, and Ruth Rose followed Ben and Josephine. With Pal at their side, they headed for the west side of Green Lawn.

It was Christmas vacation, and the store windows on Main Street were decorated with tiny white lights. Snow covered the grass, but the streets and sidewalks had been cleared.

"Is your brother home from college?" Dink asked Ben.

Ben nodded. "He came home a couple days ago."

"We bought a Christmas tree and presents!" Josephine added.

The kids crossed Main Street and

headed up Bridge Lane. They turned left and stopped at 33 Robin Road.

The house was tall and blue. Kids' toys and sports stuff were scattered across the yard and front porch.

The five kids tromped up the steps. Josephine threw open the front door and clumped down the hall, leaving snow tracks on the floor.

Dink and the rest of the kids knocked the snow off their boots before stepping inside. Josh told Pal to wait on the front porch.

"Lucky's in the kitchen," Ben said, leading the way.

Lucky was making lunch for his six brothers and sisters. Lined up on the counter were six grilled-cheese sandwiches, six glasses of milk, and six bananas.

"We brought 'em!" Josephine said. She and Ben hung up their jackets and sat at the table with the rest of their sisters and brothers.

Lucky had grown taller since Dink had last seen him. His hair was longer, too.

"Hey," Lucky said, nodding at Dink, Josh, and Ruth Rose. To his brothers and sisters, he said, "Okay, you guys eat your lunches. Be good, and no fighting! Ben's in charge."

"Why does *he* get to be in charge?" Josephine piped up.

"Because I said so," Lucky said. Then he smiled at Josephine. "You can be Ben's assistant, okay?"

Lucky beckoned for Dink, Josh, and Ruth Rose to follow him. Stepping over soccer balls, mittens, books, and hockey sticks, they trailed after Lucky into the living room.

A tall Christmas tree stood in one corner, half decorated. Ornaments and strings of lights covered the floor.

Lucky threw himself into a chair and rubbed the top of his head. "Someone robbed us," he said.

Dink looked around the room. "What did they take?" he asked.

"Lottery tickets," Lucky said. "Every year, my grandfather sends us kids a Christmas card with seven lottery tickets inside. Every year, he uses our birthdays for the numbers. And every Christmas morning, we open the card while he's here. It's a big ritual in my family. Nobody ever wins, but Gramps gets a kick out of it."

Lucky pointed to a row of Christmas cards propped up on the fireplace mantel. "This year, a burglar got in here and stole his card. I hadn't even opened the envelope!"

"But how did the burglar know there were lottery tickets inside?" Josh asked.

"I don't know," Lucky said. "My

grandfather called me this morning, all excited. He said he'd been reading his Sunday newspaper and saw that the winning lottery number was my birthday! But when I ran in here to get the card, it was gone."

"So the burglar must have learned the winning number before your grandfather did," Ruth Rose said.

Lucky nodded. "Lottery winners are announced on TV every Saturday night," he said. "The crook must've heard about it then."

"So he snuck in here last night," Josh said, "after he saw it on TV. Did he break a window or anything?"

"Wouldn't have to," Lucky said. "The back-door lock hasn't worked in years. The guy walked right in!"

"Um, how much was the ticket worth?" Dink asked.

Lucky drooped lower into his chair. "Seven big ones," he said.

"Seven thousand dollars?" Josh squeaked.

"No," Lucky said, shaking his head. "Seven million."

CHAPTER 2

Dink stared at Lucky. No one moved or spoke. Giggling and eating-lunch noises came from the kitchen.

"Seven m-million dollars!" Josh said, finally finding his voice.

Lucky nodded. "Gramps was so happy he could hardly talk," he said. "But when I told him the card was gone, I thought he was going to cry."

Lucky scooted forward in his chair.

"Do you guys think you can find the crook and get my ticket back? I can't leave the house because I have to watch the kids."

"What if it's too late?" Ruth Rose asked. "Maybe the thief cashed in the ticket already!"

Lucky shook his head. "He can't. Today's Sunday, so the lottery place is closed. But he could do it when they open again tomorrow morning."

Just then they heard a crash from the kitchen. Whispering followed the crash, then a chorus of giggling.

"Guess I better get back in there," Lucky said. "I promised I'd take them sledding after lunch. So do you think you can help?"

"Sure we'll help!" Dink said.

Lucky grinned. "Great, I—"

A three-foot-tall redhead whirled into the room. "Stuart mushed my banana!" the kid wailed. "And I didn't do nothin' to him!"

"Don't cry, Freddie. We'll make Stuie clean up that mushy banana," Lucky said. He took Freddie by the hand and headed for the kitchen. "Call me, okay?" he said over his shoulder.

The kids let themselves out. Pal was asleep on the front porch, making little snoring sounds.

"So how are we supposed to find this crook?" Josh asked. "Where do we even start?"

From the porch, Dink looked over the front yard. The snow had been trampled where the O'Leary kids had been playing.

"If the crook was here last night, maybe he left a trail," Dink said. "Let's check out back."

The kids tramped around to the back of the house. The O'Leary kids had played only in the front yard, so the snow in the back was fresh and smooth. The yard was surrounded by tall pine trees.

"Look," Josh said. A trail of footprints led to the back door from across the yard.

"The guy must've come out of those trees!" Dink said.

"And gone back the same way," Ruth Rose said. "These footprints go in both directions."

The kids followed the tracks into the trees. The footprints veered off to the right, and the kids went with them.

With his nose in the snow, Pal sniffed each footprint. Suddenly, he let out a woof.

Josh stooped down and picked something shiny out of the snow.

"What is it?" Ruth Rose asked.

Josh held out his mitten. He was

holding a piece of tinfoil that had been
twisted into the shape of a small bow
tie.

"Do you suppose the burglar
dropped this?" Josh asked.

"Keep it," Dink said. "It's our first
clue."

A few minutes later, they walked out of the woods onto Bridge Lane.

"No more footprints," Josh said, glancing up and down the lane. "The thief could've walked anywhere from here."

"Or driven," Ruth Rose said. "Maybe the guy parked a car here, then hiked into the woods."

The day was growing colder. A few big snowflakes started to fall. All three kids had pink cheeks and runny noses.

"Let's get some hot chocolate at Ellie's," Dink suggested. "Then we can plan what to do next."

It was a short hike down Bridge Lane to Ellie's Diner on Main Street. The kids pushed through the door and stomped their snowy boots on Ellie's rubber mat. Pal waddled along at Josh's heels.

"Hey, kids. Hey, Pal. What'll it be?"

Ellie asked from behind her counter.

The kids slid into a booth. "Hot chocolate," Josh said, struggling out of his down jacket. "With about a mile of whipped cream on top!"

While they waited, Dink thought about what Lucky had told them.

"Guys, anyone watching TV Saturday night would know the winning numbers, right?" he said. "But how did the thief know that the winning ticket was inside Lucky's Christmas card?"

Just then Ellie came over. "Hot stuff!" she said, setting three tall mugs on the table. Each was topped with a small mountain of whipped cream and dotted with chocolate sprinkles.

"Don't burn that cute nose, Josh," Ellie added as she turned away.

Josh blushed, then licked the top of his whipped cream.

Dink blew on his hot chocolate. "Anyone got an idea?" he asked.

"Somehow, the thief knew Lucky's grandfather mailed that ticket to Lucky," Josh said.

"But *how?*" asked Ruth Rose.

"Maybe the thief knows Lucky's grandfather," said Josh. "Maybe they're friends!"

"That's a great idea, Josh!" Ruth Rose said. "Why don't we talk to Lucky's grandfather?"

Dink fished in his pocket for a quarter. "Let me out, guys," he said. "I'm gonna call Lucky."

Dink climbed over Josh's legs. "Drink fast," he said, "but don't burn that cute nose!"

CHAPTER 3

"Got it," Dink said when he returned a few minutes later. "Lucky's grandfather is Hector O'Leary. He lives at Atrium, the elderly-housing building. Let's go see him."

"My mom says it's not good to drink too fast," Josh muttered. He licked his whipped-cream mustache and slid out of the booth. "Makes you burp," he added with a burp.

The kids headed down Main Street. Snow was falling steadily, and the sidewalk was turning white. Pal tried to bite the flakes as they fell past his nose.

The windows of the elderly-housing building were decorated with wreaths. A sign on the door said:

WELCOME TO ATRIUM—

GOOD LIVING

FOR GOOD PEOPLE

Inside the lobby, a Christmas tree stood in the center of the floor. Christmas carols came from a CD player.

"Can I help you?" A white-haired woman in a wheelchair came wheeling up to them.

"We're here to see Mr. O'Leary," Dink said.

The woman smiled. "Hector's in the atrium," she said, pointing. "Just go through the swinging doors and look for a guy wearing a yellow baseball cap. But your doggy has to wait here. I'll watch him for you."

"Thanks," Josh said, handing over the leash. "His name's Pal, and he's real friendly."

The woman leaned down and patted Pal's head. "I could tell that just by looking at him," she said.

The kids headed for the swinging doors. A note on one door said DON'T LET THE BIRDS OUT!

"Birds?" Josh said. "What birds?"

Dink shrugged. He pushed open one of the heavy wooden doors, and the kids entered the atrium.

The room felt warm and moist, like a tropical rain forest. Sunlight poured in through the glass ceiling and walls. In one corner, a fountain bubbled over smooth stones. Everywhere the kids looked they saw plants. Most were in

hanging pots, but others stood in large tubs. One tree grew right through an opening in the floor. Its branches and leaves were like a huge green umbrella.

Among the plants flew scores of parakeets. With their green, blue, and yellow feathers, they looked like flying jewels.

"This is awesome!" Josh said, ducking as a parakeet flew past his head. He took off his jacket, hat, and mittens.

Dink removed his coat as he looked around the room. Elderly men and women were feeding the birds, playing cards, or just snoozing. He saw one man with a parakeet on his head!

"I see a yellow cap," Ruth Rose said, pointing to a man standing at a workbench. The kids walked over.

Hector O'Leary wore a baggy sweatshirt and old jeans. He was nailing the roof onto a small bird-house. He looked up when the kids approached.

"Well, hello there!" Hector said. "Are you selling candy? I'll buy one of each!"

Dink shook his head. "We're friends of Lucky's," Dink said. "He told us about the lottery ticket you sent him."

The man's friendly eyes suddenly turned fiery. "I'm so mad I could spit!" he said. "What's this world coming to when burglars steal Christmas cards! If I get my hands on that gangster, he'll wish he never met Hector Francis O'Leary!"

"Lucky asked us to try to find out who stole it," Ruth Rose said. "Can we ask you some questions?"

"Okey-dokey," Hector said, laying down his hammer. "Follow me."

Lucky's grandfather led them to a circle of chairs around a low table. A blue parakeet landed on the table, carrying a small nail in his beak.

"Now, where did you get that?"
Hector took the nail and put it in his
pocket. "Blue Boy loves anything
shiny," he said. "Okey-dokey, ask away."

"Someone knew that you sent
lottery tickets to Lucky's house," Dink
said. "We were wondering if you told
anyone, like a friend."

"Well, of course I told someone!"
Hector said. He waved his arm toward
the other people in the atrium. "I told
everyone!"

CHAPTER 4

Josh glanced around at the old folks. "Could one of them be the thief?" he whispered.

Hector nodded, then put his finger to his lips. "See that woman knitting?" He dipped his chin toward a white-haired woman sitting on a sofa.

"That's Zelda Zoot," he whispered. "She's a real snoop! Has to know everyone's business around here. I know for a fact that she snitches cookies off the snack cart!"

The kids followed Hector's gaze. Zelda Zoot was a grandmotherly woman with a lap full of pink yarn and flashing knitting needles.

"Zelda hates me," he went on, "'cause I told the chef about the cookies. If anyone in this place wants to get even with me, it's Zelda."

Dink tried to picture this elderly woman tromping through the snow to burglarize Lucky's house. He couldn't do it.

"I'll keep an eye on her," Hector whispered. "If she starts acting rich, I'll let you know!"

Blue Boy suddenly flew to the top of Ruth Rose's head. He began pecking gently at her red headband.

"He likes bright colors," Hector explained.

Josh pulled a pencil out of his pocket. "Do you have some paper I could borrow?" he asked. "I have to draw a picture of Ruth Rose with a bird on her head!"

Hector chuckled and got up to get some paper.

"Don't move, Ruth Rose," Josh whispered.

"What's it doing up there?" Ruth Rose asked.

"I think he's making a nest," Dink said, grinning.

Hector came back with a sheet of paper. Josh began drawing while Ruth Rose sat like a statue.

While Josh was busy sketching, Dink thought about what Hector had told them. Any one of the Atrium's residents *could* be the thief, but Dink didn't think so.

"Mr. O'Leary, can you tell us where you bought the lottery tickets?" Dink asked.

"Sure," Hector said, dragging his chair closer to Dink. "I got 'em at the supermarket Friday morning."

"Were there any other customers around?"

Hector closed his eyes, then

snapped them open again. "Yep, I remember now. A bunch of people were standing around gabbing about the snow. Buying candy and gum. Some were behind me in line to buy lottery tickets."

"Could one of them have seen the numbers you picked?"

"I suppose it's possible," Hector said. "I wrote all my grandkids' birthdays down and handed the slip to the clerk. Then she typed the numbers into the lottery machine, and out popped the seven tickets. Anyone could have seen the numbers as I wrote them down."

Dink thought for a minute. "And did you mention that you were going to send them to your grandkids?"

Suddenly, Hector's face turned white. "I guess maybe I did," he said, "while I was addressing the envelope and putting the tickets inside. Never thought it would do any harm 'cause I never expected them to win."

Hector sighed and shook his head. "Me and my big mouth! I just can't help bragging about 'em. How I eat supper at their house, how Lucky's doin' in college, stuff like that."

Blue Boy left Ruth Rose's head and zipped across the room. He landed on one of the hanging pots.

"Rats," Josh muttered. "I hardly got started."

"Let me see," Ruth Rose said, reaching for the paper.

Josh grinned and folded the drawing in half, then slipped it into his pocket. "Nope. Not till it's done."

Dink stood up. "Thanks a lot, Mr. O'Leary," he said. "I think we'll go talk to the lottery clerk. Do you know her name?"

"Sure do," Hector said. "It's Dorothy. She's new, but she'll remember me. And if you catch the snake who stole those tickets, there'll be something extra in your Christmas stockings this year!"

"Great," Josh said. "I usually just get boring underwear!"

The kids said good-bye and left the atrium. Pal was sleeping under a potted palm tree with his leash on his paws. Josh woke him up, and the kids got back into their hats and coats.

Outside on Main Street, the wind blew snow into the kids' faces.

"Do you guys think Zelda Zoot is the thief?" Josh asked. "She looks like my grandmother!"

"If the old folks at the Atrium know that Hector sends lottery tickets to his grandkids every Christmas," Ruth Rose said, "they're all suspects!"

"Guys," Dink said, "you heard what Hector said. He likes to talk about his grandkids. *Anyone* in Green Lawn could be the thief!"

The kids trudged up Main Street. Two minutes later, they bustled into the supermarket and headed toward the lottery counter.

"Heel," Josh told Pal, who waddled along next to him.

"I wonder if that's Dorothy," Ruth Rose said. She pointed at a young blond woman behind the counter. On the wall above her head hung a small security camera.

Dink approached the counter. "Excuse me," he said. "Are you Dorothy?"

The woman looked up, chomping on a wad of gum. "That's me," she said, pointing to her name tag. It said DOROTHY CALM.

"People call me Dot. Who are you?"

"I'm Dink," he said, "and this is Josh and Ruth Rose."

Dot Calm blew a small pink bubble, let it pop, and then continued chewing. "Nice to meetcha," she said.

"We were wondering if you remember selling a bunch of lottery tickets on Friday morning," Ruth Rose said.

The woman laughed. "Kiddo, I sell hundreds of tickets every day."

"This was seven tickets together," Dink explained. He told Dot Calm about Lucky's grandfather, and how the tickets had been stolen from Lucky's house.

Dot stared at Dink for a moment, then smiled fondly. "Yeah, I remember him," she said. "Nice old gent, loves to blah, blah, blah. He told me all about his grandkids and how he sends them lottery tickets every year."

"Do you remember who was hanging around here when he bought the tickets?" Josh asked.

Dot Calm unwrapped a piece of gum and popped it into her mouth. She chewed for a few seconds, then said, "Lots of people were standing around."

"Did you notice anyone real close who could have overheard what Mr.

O'Leary was saying?" Ruth Rose asked.

Dot Calm squinted and looked into the distance. "Yeah," she said finally. "There *was* one guy I remember special." She shuddered. "He was pretty creepy-looking."

"Can you describe him?" Ruth Rose asked.

Dot Calm smiled. "I can do better than that," she said. "I know his name!"

CHAPTER 5

"You know who he is?" Dink asked.

"Just his first name," Dot Calm said. "He was wearing a bowling shirt with 'Joe' stitched over the pocket."

"Now we're getting somewhere!" Josh said.

"I think the name of his team was printed on the back of his shirt," Dot added. "I noticed it when he left, but he was too far away to read it."

Josh pulled out his pencil and flipped over the piece of drawing paper Hector had given him. "I can sketch him if you tell me what he looked like," he said.

"You can?" Dot asked. "Okay, let me see. His hair was dark and kind of floppy. He had a little mustache, too, a skinny one. And he had a space between his two front teeth."

"About how old was he?" Ruth Rose asked as Josh sketched.

Dot closed her eyes and snapped her bubble gum. "I'd say about twenty-five or so," she said finally.

"Did he have any scars or tattoos or anything?" Dink asked, watching the thief's face take shape on Josh's paper.

Dot shook her head. "Not that I can remember."

Josh held up his drawing so Dot Calm could see it. "Does that look like the guy?" he asked.

"Yeah, pretty much," she said. "But you drew his chin too square. He had kind of a pointy chin."

Josh erased the man's chin, made a few more pencil marks, and then showed her the drawing again.

"That's him!" she said. "Boy, you could make a living as an artist!"

Josh blushed. "Thanks, that's what I want to do when I grow up."

Ruth Rose looked at Dink and Josh. "We should take this to the police station and show it to Officer Fallon," she said.

"Good idea," Dink said.

The kids thanked Dot Calm and started to leave.

"Hey, I just thought of something," she called after them. "Joe said he was thinking of moving to California if he ever got enough money."

"Thanks," Dink said. "We'll tell Officer Fallon." They hurried out of the supermarket.

Snow was still falling. The wind blew it into their faces, and flakes caught on their eyelashes. Josh slipped his drawing inside his jacket to keep it dry.

A few minutes later they tapped on

Officer Fallon's door inside the police station.

"Come on in," he said. "How about a Christmas goody?" He held out a paper plate of cookies.

"We want to report a crime," Dink said, taking a cookie and sitting on one of the chairs in the office.

Josh and Ruth Rose each took one, then sat next to Dink. Josh broke his cookie in half and gave a chunk to Pal.

Officer Fallon leaned on his elbows. "I'm listening," he said.

Dink told him about the lottery tickets stolen from Lucky's house.

Officer Fallon let out a low whistle when Dink said "seven million dollars."

Ruth Rose continued, telling Officer Fallon about visiting Lucky's grandfather. And Josh finished by telling about their talk with Dot Calm. He slid his drawing out from under his jacket and showed it to Officer Fallon. "She told us his name is Joe," he said.

"Pretty good artwork, Josh," Officer Fallon said, studying the drawing. "You know, this face looks familiar."

"Do you think we can find him before tomorrow?" Dink asked.

Officer Fallon raised one eyebrow. "I can't trace him without knowing his last name," he said. "Why the rush?"

"Because tomorrow he can cash in Lucky's lottery ticket," Ruth Rose said.

"And the lottery lady said the guy is heading for California!" Josh added.

Officer Fallon stood up. "I'll do my best. Josh, can I keep this sketch?"

"Well, I was planning to finish drawing Ruth Rose," he said. "I started a picture on the back."

Officer Fallon flipped the paper over. He grinned at Ruth Rose. "Is that a bird on your head?"

"It's a parakeet," Ruth Rose said, then explained about Blue Boy.

Dink told Officer Fallon about Zelda Zoot. "Hector said she steals cookies," he added.

"We'll check her out," Officer Fallon said, heading for the copying machine.

He placed Josh's drawing on the machine, made a copy, and handed the original back to Josh.

"I'll circulate the sketch and see what turns up," he said.

"What happens if you don't find the crook in time?" Dink asked.

"Well, that's a problem," Officer Fallon said. "As far as I know, whoever presents a winning lottery ticket gets the money, no questions asked."

"Even if they stole it?" Josh said. "That's not fair!"

"I know it isn't fair," Officer Fallon said. "But the lottery people have to award the money to the ticket holder."

Officer Fallon thought for a minute. "I suppose if they had proof that the ticket was stolen, they would hold back the money." He looked at the kids. "But you have no real proof. Your friend can't prove his grandfather bought the tickets or sent them."

Dink stood up. "Then we'll get proof!" he said.

CHAPTER 6

The kids thanked Officer Fallon and left. "Let's go to my house and talk," Dink said as they stepped outside into the falling snow.

"Talk, schmalk," Josh sputtered. "I've gotta eat lunch! That half a cookie made me hungry!"

Dink laughed. "Okay, we'll eat while we figure out what to do next."

By the time they reached Dink's

front door, they looked like three kid-sized snowmen. They left their jackets, boots, hats, and mittens in the hall and headed for the kitchen.

Pal trotted in and immediately flopped down next to the radiator.

Dink found a note from his mom on the table.

Dink,

I had to take the car in for snow tires. Heat up the soup in the microwave and make peanut butter sandwiches. I'll be home soon.

Love, Mom

"I'll make the sandwiches," Josh said, pawing through the cupboard.

Dink heated some tomato soup, and the kids carried their lunches into the den. "Anyone want to watch a video?" Dink asked.

"Video!" Ruth Rose said suddenly.

"That's it!"

"What's it?" Josh asked.

"There was a video camera at the lottery counter," Ruth Rose said. "If Joe's bowling team is on the back of his shirt, maybe it'll show up on the tape!"

"Good idea!" Dink said. "I'd better tell Officer Fallon."

He picked up the phone and called the police station. After Dink told Officer Fallon about the video camera, he dialed information and asked for the phone number of the supermarket. Dink dialed again and asked to be transferred to Dot Calm at the lottery counter.

Dink asked Dot if the camera was turned on the day Hector bought the seven tickets. He listened, said thank you, and then hung up.

"She's gonna ask her boss to check the tape," Dink said. "If the name of

Joe's bowling team shows up, Dot's boss will call Officer Fallon."

"I wonder if this Joe guy bowls at the fitness center," Josh said.

"Good thinking, Josh," Dink said. "We can check it out after we eat."

"What's *this?*" Ruth Rose suddenly cried. Something had fallen out of her hair and landed in her soup.

Josh giggled. "Maybe it's a cootie."

"No, Joshua, it's not a cootie!" Ruth Rose said. She lifted something shiny onto her soup spoon. "It's another tinfoil bow tie!"

Josh dug the other bow tie out of his pocket. Except that one was wet from tomato soup, the two tinfoil bow ties were the same.

Ruth Rose looked at Dink and Josh. "How did that thing get in my hair?" she asked.

The kids stared at each other. "Blue Boy!" they shouted at the same time.

"He must've had it in his beak when he landed on your head," Dink said. "He buried it in your hair!"

"Yeah, but where did he get it?" Josh asked.

"The bow tie had to be in the atrium," Dink said. "Those parakeets never go outside."

"Then the crook must have been in the atrium, too!" Ruth Rose said. "Maybe it *is* Zelda Zoot!"

"It could still be Joe," Josh said. "He might've gone to the atrium to ask someone where Hector's grandkids live."

Just then Dink's mother burst into the house. "The roads are awful, and it's still snowing!" she said.

She slipped off her coat, scarf, and boots. "This will be a good night to curl up with a big bowl of popcorn."

"That's what we do after skiing," Ruth Rose said.

"You know how to ski?" Josh asked.

"Sure. My family learned to cross-country-ski a couple years ago," Ruth Rose said. "Hey, why don't I teach you guys? We can get around town a lot easier that way."

"That's a nice idea," Dink's mother said. "Just keep out of the streets. The snowplows are out in full force."

The kids cleaned up their lunch things, got into their jackets, and walked next door to Ruth Rose's house.

She took three sets of cross-country skis and poles from the garage. Then she showed Dink and Josh how to strap them onto their boots.

"Okay, now just glide," she said. "Slide your skis along the snow and use the poles to keep your balance."

"Piece of cake," Josh said, taking a step.

He fell into a snowbank.

CHAPTER 7

Soon Dink and Josh could follow Ruth Rose across her backyard without falling.

"You guys learned fast," she said. "Why don't we ski to the fitness center? We can show Josh's picture around in the bowling alley."

The kids skied around the school. Pal bounded after them, leaping high in the snow.

When they reached Main Street, they waited for a snowplow to pass, then skied across to the other side.

They stopped near the corner of Bridge Lane and Main. A man carrying a heavy-looking satchel and a pair of snowshoes came out of the fitness center.

The man smiled at the kids. "Nice day to be out in the snow," he said.

"We just learned how to ski," Josh said.

The man flopped his snowshoes onto the snowy sidewalk and tried to strap them onto his boots with one hand.

"Can I hold your bag for you?" Dink asked.

"Thanks," the man said. "Don't drop it on your toe, it's my bowling ball."

"Do you belong to a bowling team?" Josh asked.

"Yep. I bowl with the Green Lawn Giants," he said. "Why, you thinking of joining a kids' league?"

"No, but we were wondering if you know this guy." Josh pulled out his drawing of Joe and showed it to the man.

"Hmmm," the man said, studying the picture. "He's not on our team, but he looks familiar."

"His name is Joe," Ruth Rose said.

The man shook his head and clicked his tongue. "I'm pretty sure I've seen this face before," he said. "Why don't you ask inside?"

"Thanks, we will," Dink said.

The man finished strapping on his snowshoes and took back his bowling bag. "Thanks for your help," he said, then clomped down Main Street.

The kids brushed the snow off a bench and sat to remove their skis. They carried the skis and poles into the fitness center and walked down a set of stairs. Pal trotted right behind them.

Two long bowling lanes took up most of the basement. A bunch of men and women were bowling. Some of them wore shirts with names over the pockets.

There was a cart in one corner where a woman sold hot dogs and sodas.

Josh and Pal stopped and stared at the cart. "Why don't we get some lunch?" Josh asked.

"We ate lunch, remember?" Dink said, glancing around.

"Do you see Joe anywhere?" Ruth Rose asked.

Dink shook his head. Not one of the men looked like Josh's sketch.

"Let's ask if anyone knows him," Josh said.

The kids leaned their skis and poles in a corner and left Pal in charge. They began showing Josh's picture to anyone who wasn't bowling.

A few people said Joe looked like someone they'd seen.

One woman said Joe resembled her husband, George.

A man said Joe had a face like a bank robber he'd seen on a MOST WANTED sign at the post office.

But no one said they *knew* Joe.

"Well, that was a big waste of time," Josh muttered.

On the way out of the basement, the kids passed the hot dog stand. Josh unfolded his drawing. "Have you seen this guy?" he asked the woman.

She laughed. "Are you trying to be cute with me, sonny boy?"

"What do you mean?" Josh asked.

"I mean," the woman said, tapping the drawing with one finger, "this is a picture of you, only older."

The kids took a closer look at the sketch.

"She's right!" Ruth Rose said. "It *does* look like Josh, except for the mustache."

"That's why everyone said this guy looks familiar," Dink said. "He looks just like you!"

Josh stared at his drawing. "So there is no Joe?"

The woman behind the cart had been listening. "Sounds like you've been sent on a wild-goose chase," she said.

"But why would Dot have us looking for some guy who isn't even real?" Josh asked. "I don't get it."

Dink shrugged. "I don't, either," he said. "Why don't we ask her? The supermarket is right across the street."

CHAPTER 8

The kids carried their skis across Bridge Lane and into the supermarket. The store was almost empty on this snowy Sunday afternoon.

"Look," Dink said, pointing to a small sign taped to the lottery machine:

CLOSED FOR THE STORM.

SEE YOU TOMORROW.

Just then a teenager walked by. He

was carrying a broom and a dustpan. The name tag on his shirt said ERIC.

"Cool pooch," he said, smiling at Pal.

"Do you know if Dot is still here?" Ruth Rose asked.

"Nope," the kid said. "She left a while ago, all happy. She goes, like, 'Merry Christmas, Eric!' and slips me twenty bucks. I go, like, 'Wow, thanks, Dot!'"

Eric walked behind the counter.

"What a mess Dot left back here," he mumbled as he began sweeping.

"Um, do you know if Dot's boss is around?" Dink said. "Can we talk to him?"

Eric crouched down behind the counter. "It's a her, not a him," he said, standing up. "The boss is Mrs. Milk. She's, like, out sick, though. She's had the flu all week."

"The flu?" Dink said. "But Dot told
me she'd talk to—"

Suddenly, Pal let out a howl. He
buried his nose in the pile of dust Eric
had swept up.

"What did you find?" Josh asked. "Let me have it, boy." Josh pried open Pal's mouth and pulled something out.

"Look, guys!" Josh held out a small tinfoil bow tie.

Ruth Rose took it from Josh, then pulled the other two out of her pocket.

The three were exactly the same.

The kids leaned over the counter. The floor was littered with tiny tinfoil bow ties.

Suddenly, it all made sense. Dink could tell by the looks on their faces that Josh and Ruth Rose had figured it out, too.

"Come on," Dink muttered. He grabbed his skis and poles and hurried toward the exit.

Josh and Ruth Rose followed with their skis and poles. "Let's go, Pal," Josh told his dog.

"Are you guys thinking what I'm

thinking?" Ruth Rose asked once they were outside.

"Yeah," Dink muttered. "Boy, have we been dopes! Let's go back to Ellie's." They trudged through the snow and piled into the diner.

Ellie looked up. "Twice in one day?" she said. "Three more hot chocolates?"

"Thanks, Ellie," Dink said. The kids slid into a booth while Pal flopped down at their feet.

"So Dot Calm is the crook, right?" Josh said.

"Right," Dink said. "After Dot sold Hector his tickets, she must have kept the paper he wrote the kids' birthdays on. That's how she knew Lucky's ticket was the winner."

"But she didn't know where Lucky lived," Ruth Rose said, "so she had to go to the Atrium to find out. She wouldn't want to talk to Hector, so she probably asked someone else where his grandkids lived. She must've dropped a bow tie while she was snooping!"

"Then she went to Lucky's house and stole the card...," Dink added.

"...and dropped another bow tie in the snow," Josh said.

"Then she made up that story about Joe to throw us off her trail," Ruth Rose said.

Dink looked at Josh. "I bet she described your face because she was looking right at you when you were drawing him."

"Yeah, and I was so dumb I didn't even notice it was me," Josh said.

"Here we go, kids." Ellie brought their hot chocolates to the table. "These are on me, and a little treat for Pal."

Ellie set a bowl of chopped-up hamburger in front of Pal's nose. Pal raised his head, blinked his big brown eyes at Ellie, and stuck his nose in the bowl.

"Thanks a lot, Ellie," Josh said. "Pal says thanks, too."

Ruth Rose had been sipping her hot chocolate. "You know, guys," she said, "we can't *prove* Dot stole the tickets. We *know* she did it, but Officer Fallon will say, 'Where's the proof?'"

Dink nodded. "Yeah, that's *exactly* what he'll say."

"Well, unless we find the proof," Josh said, "this sure is going to be a lousy Christmas for Lucky's family. Seven million bucks down the drain."

The kids drank their hot chocolate with glum expressions on their faces.

From beneath the table came the sound of happy chomping.

CHAPTER 9

Dink invited Josh and Ruth Rose to spend the night. They unrolled their sleeping bags in front of Dink's Christmas tree. Pal crawled inside Josh's bag and started snoring.

While it snowed outside, the kids tried to figure out how to prove that Dot Calm had stolen Lucky's lottery ticket.

"If only we had a witness," Ruth Rose said from her sleeping bag.

"Too bad she didn't drop something with her name on it," Josh offered, warming his feet on Pal's body.

"That would be too easy," Dink mumbled. He crawled into his sleeping bag and closed his eyes.

Then Dink was dreaming. But it wasn't a happy, the-night-before-Christmas-Eve kind of dream.

This was a nightmare. Dink was outside somewhere, floundering in the snow. He was barefoot, without gloves, and freezing. His tracks crisscrossed each other as he tried to find his way home.

Dink yelled and sat up. From inside Josh's sleeping bag, Pal whimpered.

"It's okay," Dink whispered. He sat and thought for a minute, then crawled out of his bag. He tiptoed up the stairs and came down with his alarm clock. In the hall, Dink made a phone call, left a quiet message, and returned to the living room.

He set the alarm for six o'clock and put the clock in the foot of his sleeping bag. Then Dink climbed back in and went to sleep.

When the alarm buzzed, Dink pressed the off button with his toes. He slipped out of his bag and shook Josh and Ruth Rose. "Wake up," he whispered. "And be quiet!"

Josh yawned and Ruth Rose blinked her eyes. Silently, they watched Dink pull on his boots.

Dink grinned. "Come on, you guys," he said. "Meet me in the kitchen."

"There better be breakfast," Josh mumbled.

Within minutes, the three kids were

drinking orange juice and eating toast. Josh shared his bread with Pal, who then went back to Josh's warm sleeping bag.

Dink told Josh and Ruth Rose about his nightmare. "All I could see was my footprints in the snow," he said. "When I woke up, I thought about what Josh said about wishing Dot had left something with her name on it."

He grinned. "I know how we can prove Lucky's grandfather really did buy that ticket."

"How?" Josh said. "And why'd you have to tell us this in the middle of the night?"

"Fingerprints," Dink said. "Whose fingerprints would be on that stolen ticket?"

"Dot's would be, if she stole it," Ruth Rose said.

"But her prints would be on the

ticket anyway, since she sold it to Lucky's grandfather," Josh said. "So what does that prove?"

"Nothing," Dink said. "But Dot's fingerprints aren't the only ones on that ticket..."

Josh and Ruth Rose stared at him. "You're right!" Ruth Rose said. "Hector's fingerprints are on the ticket, too!"

"Um, can they get prints off lottery tickets?" Josh asked.

Dink nodded. "I think so. I saw a program about fingerprints on TV," he said. "Fingers are oily, and the oil stains paper when we touch it."

"We should tell Officer Fallon," Ruth Rose said.

Dink nodded. "I left a message on his voice mail asking him to meet us at the lottery headquarters in Blue Hills."

"But that's two miles from here!"

Josh said. He glanced out the window. "And it's still dark out."

"We can get there fast on skis," Dink said. "And by that time, the sun will be up."

"Are they even open?" Ruth Rose asked. "I bet a lot of places are closed today because of the snow."

"I thought of that," Dink said, setting the glasses in the sink. "If the place is closed, Dot Calm won't be able to cash in the ticket. But if it's open, we'll catch her in the act!"

"Then Lucky will be a millionaire!" Josh said. "Times seven!"

"Let's get going," Dink said. "We can get to Blue Hills fastest if we ski along the river."

Dink scribbled a note to his parents, and then the kids went back to the living room and finished dressing.

Suddenly, Josh's sleeping bag

moved. A big bump wriggled toward the opening, and Pal poked his nose out. He looked at Josh and woofed.

"He wants to come with us," Josh whispered, rubbing Pal's silky ears.

The kids grabbed their skis and poles and stepped outside.

A full moon hung over Green Lawn, turning the snow to silver. The kids saw their breath as they skied out of Dink's

yard and past Ruth Rose's house. They followed River Road south toward Blue Hills.

Once they found their rhythm, the kids zipped along. Over the river, the sun slowly appeared. Silver became gold as night turned to day.

Pal trotted happily along, his breath making small clouds.

CHAPTER 10

Dink read the sign sticking out of the snowbank: WELCOME TO BLUE HILLS.

The kids stopped and leaned on their ski poles. The sun shone on the spruce trees, turning their snowy branches to gold.

"The town can't be far now," Dink said. He looked at his watch. "It's almost eight."

"Can we rest for a while?" Josh asked. "I feel like lying right down in the snow."

"We could," Dink said, "but what if Dot cashes in the ticket while we're resting?"

"She's probably still in bed," Josh grumbled, "where we should be."

Ruth Rose laughed. "Josh, would you still be in bed if you had a winning lottery ticket? Come on, I'll race you!"

Dink and Josh skied after Ruth Rose, and a few minutes later they were on Main Street in Blue Hills.

"Let's ask where the lottery place is," Ruth Rose said, pointing to a gas station.

The kids skied up to the office and peeked in the window. Dink saw a man reading a newspaper and sipping from a coffee mug.

Dink tapped on the window, and

the man got up and opened the door. "Skis," the man said. "Why didn't I think of that? My poor old truck nearly skidded into Indian River this morning!"

He knelt and patted Pal. "Bet this fella wishes he had some skis, too."

"Can you tell us how to get to the lottery place?" Dink asked.

"Sure can," the man said. He stepped outside and closed the door behind him. "See that flashing light? That's Middle Street. Hang a right there, and about a half mile up, you'll see the sign. Red-brick building."

He glanced at the kids. "One of you a winner?"

"No, but a friend of ours is!" Ruth Rose said.

The man looked at his watch. "Place must be just opening," he said.

"Thanks a lot, mister," Dink said,

and they skied up the quiet white street.

There were two cars in the parking lot in front of lottery headquarters. One of the cars had pulled in next to a sign that said EMPLOYEE PARKING. The other car was right in front of the entrance. Josh peeked through the windows.

"Guys, take a look," he whispered.

Dink and Ruth Rose skied over and looked into the car. Gum wrappers twisted into silver bow ties littered the floor and seats.

"Dot must be inside!" Ruth Rose said. "Hurry up, let's get in there!"

The kids took off their skis and left them and their poles outside the door. Josh told Pal to stay.

Dink opened the door, and the kids stepped inside. The room had a few chairs, a counter, and a row of filing cabinets.

A Christmas song was coming from a radio on a shelf. On the same shelf was perched a video camera. The lens was aimed at the counter. A small sign read: ALL LOTTERY TRANSACTIONS ARE TAPED FOR YOUR SAFETY.

A man was standing at the counter with his back to the kids. He was wearing a puffy down coat. A ski hat was pulled down over dark hair, and Dink could just see one end of a mustache.

"That guy looks like my picture of Joe!" Josh hissed in Dink's ear.

The man reached a hand into his pocket. When he pulled his hand out, something dropped to the floor. It was another silver bow tie!

Just then a clerk approached the counter. She smiled at the kids and said, "Good morning. I'll be right with you."

The man turned around, and Dink gasped. It wasn't a man at all. It was Dot Calm wearing a wig and fake mustache!

Dot Calm recognized the kids. Her eyes widened in surprise, and then she turned quickly back to the clerk.

"Here's the ticket," she said. "Now I'll take my check for seven million, please."

The clerk nodded and slid a paper across the counter. "If you'll just sign this..."

"Stop!" Dink yelled. "She's a crook, and she stole that lottery ticket!"

The clerk's mouth dropped open. "What do you mean? Who are you?"

"We're friends of the ticket's *real* owner," Ruth Rose said.

"Yeah, and we can prove it's stolen!" Josh threw in.

Dot Calm sneered at the kids. "I bought this ticket Friday, and nobody can prove I didn't."

"Yeah?" Dink retorted. "Then why are my friend's fingerprints on it?"

"Baloney," Dot Calm said through her fake mustache.

"And *your* fingerprints are on the mantel where you stole the Christmas card!" Ruth Rose said, pointing at Dot Calm.

Dot Calm laughed. "You're crazy, kid. I was wearing glov..."

The clerk picked up the telephone. "I'm calling the police," she said.

Suddenly, Dot Calm charged toward the door. She flung it open and hurtled out into the snow.

Josh ran after her, screaming, "Attack, Pal!"

When the kids got outside, Dot Calm was lying in the snow with her feet tangled in skis and ski poles. Pal was sitting on the thief's back, barking.

Suddenly, two police cruisers roared into the parking lot. Officer Fallon stepped from one of them, Officer

Keene from the other.

"What's going on?" Officer Fallon asked.

"She stole Lucky's lottery ticket," Dink said, pointing to Dot Calm. "And we have proof! Lucky's grandfather's fingerprints will be on the ticket."

Josh pulled Pal away, and Officer Fallon helped Dot Calm to her feet. Her face was covered with snow. When she wiped the snow away, the mustache fell off.

"What...who is this character?" Officer Fallon asked.

"Her name is Dot Calm," Dink said. "She's wearing a wig!"

Officer Fallon reached over and pulled at the wig. It came off, revealing Dot Calm's blond hair.

"Anything to say for yourself, miss?" Officer Fallon said.

Dot Calm shook her head.

"Then hold out your hands." Officer Fallon snapped on a pair of handcuffs. Officer Keene led Dot Calm to his cruiser.

Just then the clerk came bustling out of the office holding the lottery ticket. "What should I do with this?" she asked. "It's the seven-million-dollar winner!"

Officer Fallon looked at Dink, Josh, and Ruth Rose. "Would you kids like a ride to Lucky's house?" he asked.

Five minutes later, the cruiser pulled up in front of 33 Robin Road. The kids and Pal piled out, followed by Officer Fallon.

Lucky and his six brothers and sisters were building snow people in their front yard. They all came running over to the cruiser.

"Are you gonna 'rest us?" Josephine

asked. Her cheeks and nose were as red as her mittens.

Officer Fallon patted Josephine on her head. "No, but Dink has something to give your big brother."

Dink grinned and handed the seven-

million-dollar winning ticket to Lucky.

"Merry Christmas!" he said.

Lucky took one look at the ticket,
then fell over in the snow.

"Pig pile!" Ben O'Leary yelled, and
all six redheads leaped on top of Lucky.

Collect clues with Dink, Josh, and Ruth Rose in their next exciting adventure,

THE MISSING MUMMY

Dr. Tweed walked over to the three mummy cases. One by one, he raised each lid.

Dink heard some of the kids gasp. The mummies were shaped like human bodies. Each was wrapped in cloth that was blackened with age. A dry, musty smell seeped into the room.

"Each mummy is wrapped in strips of linen," Dr. Tweed said. "Beneath the cloth—"

Suddenly, a woman in a baggy dress darted toward the mummies. She snatched the smallest one and raced through the door leading to the treasure chamber.

"Stop!" Dr. Tweed shouted as he bolted after her.

About the Author

Ron Roy is the author of more than thiry-five books for children, including *A Thousand Pails of Water*, *Where's Buddy?*, and the award-winning *Whose Hat Is That?* He is currently writing the widely read A to Z Mysteries® series. When he's not writing, Ron spends time traveling all over the country and restoring his old Connecticut farmhouse.